To My Wife, Phobe – *M.M.*

To My Supportive Parents – *E.S.*

Inquiring Voices Press
100 Heritage Rd
Bloomington IN 47408
(812) 336-6925

Printed in Korea

ISBN 0-9634637-1-3 (hard)   ISBN 0-9634637-2-1 (soft)
Library of Congress Catalog Card Number : 96-77103

THE DAY THE EARTH WAS SILENT

Michael McGuffee, *Author*

Edward Sullivan, *Illustrator*

Inquiring Voices Press, Bloomington, Indiana

THE DAY THE EARTH WAS SILENT

Michael McGuffee, *Author*

Edward Sullivan, *Illustrator*

The class stood in silence.
They had made a new flag
Showing the blue white marble of earth,
Traveling silently through the blackness of space.

The children took the flag to their principal
And he sent it up the flag pole.

"Why not share our flag with all the earth?"
  asked one student.
"Why try?" said the principal.
"People wouldn't understand."
"But we are saying *why not try*?"
  replied another student.
"Well, I guess I don't know why not,"
  said the principal.
"Ask the mayor, she might know."

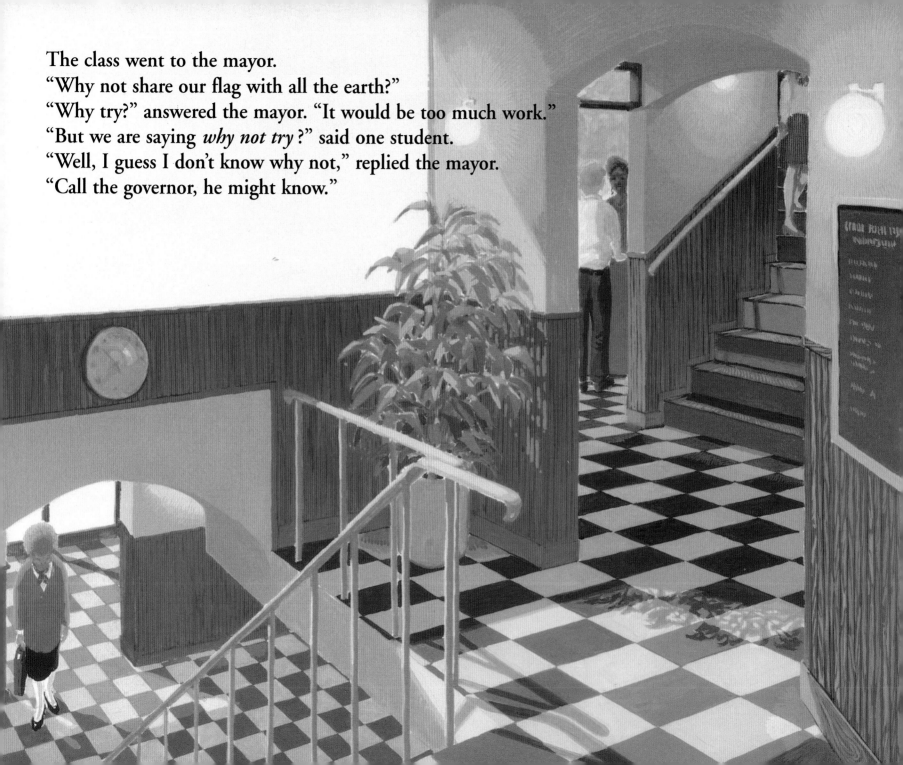

The class went to the mayor.
"Why not share our flag with all the earth?"
"Why try?" answered the mayor. "It would be too much work."
"But we are saying *why not try* ?" said one student.
"Well, I guess I don't know why not," replied the mayor.
"Call the governor, he might know."

The children called the governor.
"Why not share our flag with all the earth?"
"Why try?" said the governor. "It would cost too much."
"But we are saying *why not try* ?"
"Well, I guess I don't know why not," replied the governor.
"Call the president, she might know."

The children called the the president,
And they were allowed to ask their question.
"You have asked a very thoughtful question," said the president.
"And your question deserves a thoughtful answer.
Since the flag is for the people of the earth, we should ask them."

A meeting was set
And delegates gathered from around the world.

The class asked their question.

"We already have flags for all the people," said one delegate.

"We haven't asked you to put your flags away," said one of the children.

"Our flags speak for our great nations," said another delegate.

"Our flag speaks for our tiny earth," replied a student.

"Our flags show who we are," said a delegate.

"Our flag shows who we might become," the children responded.

The children unfolded the flag.
After a long silence, another delegate spoke.

"When you first arrived, we knew
the reasons why your idea would
never work. But after meeting you
and seeing your flag, we understand.
Your question answers itself,
indeed – why not try!"

So a day was set to raise the flag.

The earth spun,
And the sun rose.

The flag was raised,
And the people were silent.

As the earth completed a turn in space,
And the beginning of a new day
Met the ending of the old,
For one timeless moment
All the earth was silent.

And the silence was healing.

The flag served its purpose,
And the people knew.
So the children put the flag away,
And it eventually was forgotten.

But the healing silence
Was treasured
Forever.

The flag served its purpose,
And the people knew.
So the children put the flag away,
And it eventually was forgotten.

But the healing silence
Was treasured
Forever.

Dedicated to Christa McAuliffe,
who wanted to see the earth whole.

MICHAEL McGUFFEE, in 1988, received the Christa McAuliffe Fellowship from the United States Department of Education, which allowed him to provide staff development to teachers around Oklahoma. The story of *The Day The Earth Was Silent* grew out of his work in classrooms during the fellowship.

Michael and his family live in Stillwater, Oklahoma, where he writes and teaches. He has written numerous children's books and is currently working as senior editor of *Homeplay*, a collection of picture books devoted to fostering family literacy.

EDWARD SULLIVAN currently lives in Boston. *The Day The Earth Was Silent* is his first children's book.

"The love of drawing is the most important feature of my work. I fill my sketch books with buildings, trees, and most of all people in action."